D1076642

WICKED!

Janet Paisley

SANDSTONE vista 9

The Sandstone Vista Series

Wicked!

First published 2006 in Great Britain by Sandstone Press Ltd
PO Box 5725, Dingwall, Ross-shire, IV15 9WJ, Scotland

Sandstone Press gratefully acknowledges the ongoing support
of Highland Council, Highland Adult Literacy Partnership,
and Essex County Council Libraries

ISBN-10: 1-905207-07-7
ISBN-13: 978-1-905207-07-7

The Sandstone Vista Series of books has
been written and skilfully edited
for the enjoyment of readers with differing levels
of reading skills, from the emergent to the accomplished.

Designed and typeset by Edward Garden Graphic Design,
Dingwall, Ross-shire, Scotland.

Printed and bound by Bell and Bain, Glasgow, Scotland.

SANDSTONEPRESS
CONTEMPORARY QUALITY READING
www.sandstonepress.com

WICKED
Janet Paisley

Jas overhears his wife in bed with an Italian.
His plan to retire early and spend their winters
in Italy is out the window. He tries to confront
Linda but it all goes wrong. Is she toying with
him? She's toying with lots of other things –
Italians, sexy underwear, massage oil. Jas tries
to end it all but that goes wrong too. Is his life
over? Or has he got the wrong end of the stick?
Just when things can't get worse, worse
is what they get.

Janet Paisley is the award-winning author of five
books of poetry, two fiction books and many
plays, radio, TV and film scripts. She grew up in
Avonbridge, near Falkirk, is the single parent of
six grown-up sons and is a first-time grannie.
Her writing is used in schools and universities in
Russia, Europe and America.

By the same author

Fiction
Not for Glory
Wild Fire

Poetry
Ye Cannae Win
Reading the Bones
Alien Crop
Biting through Skins
Pegasus in Flight
Images - video

Drama
Double Yella
Straitjackets
Winding String
Deep Rising
Refuge
Silver Bullet - radio
Diary of a Goth - radio
Curds and Cream - radio
Long Haul - film

With Graham McKenzie
Sooans Nicht
For Want of a Nail
Bill and Koo - radio

For Janice and Linda, for wickedness
and the fun of it

CHAPTER ONE

Life was good. Birds were singing. The sun was shining. Jas was a happy man. He drove his white van into the village and up the slope beside his shop, whistling. It was an old tune. A song sung by the American singer, Burl Ives. It was a song about a bluebird on his shoulder. *My, oh my, what a wonderful day*, it went. Jas couldn't remember all the words. But he could remember the tune. So he whistled it as he got out of the van, locked it and felt in his jacket pocket for the shop keys.

No keys. He felt in his other pocket. No keys there either. He felt in his trouser pockets. Nope, no keys. He unlocked the van and checked. No keys on the passenger seat. No keys in the door pocket. He felt in his jacket pockets again, just in case. No, no keys. He got back in the van. Home was just a mile up the hill in the next village. It was a fine morning. The sun was shining. He'd be ten minutes late opening the shop. Another day he'd be annoyed. Today, it didn't matter. Life was good.

Jas reversed the van back down the slope, swung it round and drove out of the village. At the main road, he turned left, drove round the bend over the canal and up the hill for home. On both sides, the trees and fields were newly green. Birds were busy doing those things birds do on fine spring mornings. Jas was a happy man.

In six months, before winter came, he'd stop work, retire. The shop would be sold. He and his wife would be free to enjoy life. First stop would be a long holiday in Italy. His daughter and her husband lived there, in Tuscany. Their house had a small separate flat. Jas and Linda could stay there any time they felt like flying out.

It would be beautiful in Tuscany in autumn. They might even stay till spring came again. They could shut their own house up for the winter. Drain the water tank and central heating. Stay away as long as they liked. The whole winter could be spent in Italy. They could come back for summer in Scotland, do the garden, visit old haunts, see old pals. That wasn't a bad plan. Not bad at all. Jas was a very happy man.

He drove up to his house still whistling. At his front door, he slid the key in the lock quietly. Linda would still be asleep. She had two hours before she started work. She was a secretary in a lawyer's office in town. In autumn, she would retire too. Early. She was only fifty five. Forty years was long enough for anybody to work, she said. She wanted to enjoy life while she still could.

Jas tiptoed into the kitchen. There they were. His shop keys. They lay on the kitchen table beside his half-drunk cup of coffee. He was sixty, retiring early too. Just as well, if he was going to be forgetful. He grinned to himself. He was still lean and slim. He was fit and still vital. Not bad for sixty, even if his memory was going.

He tiptoed back down the hall. Then he heard a moan. A long, deep moan from upstairs. Linda! Linda was in trouble. He turned and ran up the stairs. The thick carpet muffled his footsteps. He would have called out for his wife but he needed his breath to run upwards. So much for fit. At the top, he slowed, catching his breath.

'Ohhhh,' Linda moaned. Jas reached for the bedroom doorhandle. 'Ohh, Emilio,' his wife groaned. Jas froze. Emilio? Who the hell was Emilio? And then Emilio spoke.

'Cara mia,' he said, in a thick Italian accent. 'Cara mia.'

Jas jerked his hand back from the doorknob. The fear that had made him run upstairs changed. Now it was a different fear. He stepped back from the door. From behind it he could hear Linda moaning with pleasure. Behind it, he could hear the deep, throaty whispers of the man who was with her. Jas backed slowly down the thick carpeted staircase. He kept his eyes fixed on the closed bedroom door. His bedroom door. His bedroom where his wife was in bed with another man.

Heart thumping, Jas let himself back out of the house and shut the door quietly behind him. He winced as he started the van's engine. Did it have to be so loud? He gritted his teeth as he drove away, away from his home and his wife and the other man she was with. He frowned hard as he drove down the hill towards his shop. He was not whistling now. Plenty of sunshine was not coming his way. Jas was not a happy man.

CHAPTER TWO

'Who stole your scone?' Carol asked. She worked for him in the shop.

'Nobody,' Jas said. 'I'm eating it.' He was too. The scone was on the plate next his mid-morning coffee. It was half eaten. He wasn't enjoying it, even though it was a fruit scone. You couldn't enjoy a scone when your wife was cheating on you with another man. You just ate it, out of habit. You did a lot of things out of habit, even if your wife was cheating on you. Jas had been surprised how much you could do from habit.

He'd come back, opened the shop, checked the till, sorted papers, served customers. When Carol arrived, he made out she was late.

'What time d'you call this?' he asked, like he always did.

'The right time,' Carol snapped, like she

always did. She was never late. It was their little joke.

When break time came, he put the kettle on and made the coffee. He always made the coffee, even though it wasn't his turn. It was never his turn because he always did it. He always pointed this out to Carol, that it was her turn but not to worry, he'd do it. So, every day, it was her turn. Every day, he did it instead. That way, it always was her turn. It was never his turn. He liked that. It was a habit. He was a man of habit.

'Are you trying to change that into chocolate cake or make it rise up off the plate and float into your mouth?'

'What?' What was she on about?

'The scone,' Carol said. 'You're staring at it that hard, I swear it's gone pink with embarrassment. Eat it or bin it, for God's sake. I can't enjoy my coffee for watching you watching that scone!'

He binned it. So much for habit. He'd never binned a scone in his life.

'I'm going out for a walk,' he said. Another habit bit the dust. He'd never left the shop in the middle of the day before either.

He walked to the canal bridge. Not the bridge on the main road. That led home. He walked to the bridge on the old back road. Now that was habit. There weren't many places to walk to. Turn right and the road led down the hill to the town. Turn left and it led up the hill and home. Taking the fork onto the back road was the only way to get away from everything. He leaned over the bridge and stared at the black water below.

He'd been here before. Been here, staring at the water, feeling unhappy. That was years ago. The shop wasn't doing well then. Their daughter was still at university. He'd lied to Linda about the shop. Let her think business was good. It wasn't. Not then. When he couldn't get away with lying any more, he'd come down here. He'd put stones in his coat pockets. He'd filled his boots with plaster. He'd tied his wrists together with his belt. Then he'd climbed up on the bridge and jumped into the canal.

He'd landed on a barge. Went through the wooden roof. Broke both his legs. He wasn't doing that again. He hadn't been telling the lies this time. Linda had. He went back to the shop.

'Feel better?' Carol asked. She was filling the

sweet shelves.

'I feel fine,' he told her.

'Could've fooled me,' she muttered.

'Is it a lie if you don't tell somebody something?' he asked.

'Depends.'

'On what?'

'On whether it's something they should be told or not.' She stopped filling the shelf to look at him. 'What are you not telling me?'

'I'm not *not* telling you anything. Not anything that's any of your business, anyway. I mean, I was just asking.' A horrible thought struck him. Carol probably knew. Everybody probably knew. Wasn't the husband always the last to know? 'Unless there's anything you're not telling me,' he said, accusingly.

'Have you been drinking?' she said.

'Is there?'

'What?'

'Anything you're not telling me? Something you know about me that you're not saying. Something I should know and you shouldn't but you do and I don't. What is it you're not telling me?'

'That you're a nutter?'

No respect. That was Carol's problem. She had no respect.

'I just want to know what everybody else knows about me!' He was getting loud now. Outside, a customer on the way in stopped to talk to someone who was passing. They were probably talking about him, about *it*. He lowered his voice. 'I want to know what they say *about* me that they won't say *to* me.'

Carol started tearing up the empty boxes.

'Sometimes it's better not to know,' she mumbled.

So, he was right! They all knew. They were all talking about it. Talking about him! Talking about Linda and her bit on the side.

'I want to know!' He banged the glass counter. The charity box rattled. Carol jumped. She glared at him.

'You're very annoying,' she said. 'You have some very annoying habits.'

'Me?'

'Whistling,' she said. She stuck her fingers up to count them off. Good grief, she needed fingers to count them. 'Repeating yourself.'

'Me?'

'Making out I'm late every morning. Making the coffee every morning so you can look long suffering. Making silly jokes.'

'Silly jokes?' He was witty. Was that a crime? She was on to her second hand. Good grief, he had more than one handful? Then she seemed to think twice. She dropped her hands.

'You have some very annoying habits,' she finished, lamely.

'And?'

'And what?'

'There were another five. You had another five things you know about me that I don't. Things people say about me but won't say to me. What are they?'

The customer who'd been gossiping outside came in. It was Jenny Davis. Jas served. Carol went through the back. He could tell she was annoyed the way she was tearing up the rest of the empty boxes. It sounded like a Dobermann with a rabbit was in the back shop. Jenny was in for her fags.

'It's not the cough what carries you off,' Jas said as he lifted the packet down. 'It's the coffin they carry you off in.'

'They should put that on the packet,' Jenny said. 'We'd die laughing.'

At least somebody liked his jokes.

'So what's the gossip today?' he asked. He felt quite pleased at how innocent the question sounded.

'You don't want to know,' Jenny said, and left.

But he did. Now that he knew, he wanted to know how many of them knew and how long they'd known. Carol came back through. There were flakes of torn cardboard in her hair.

'And?' he asked.

'Give it a rest,' she said.

He picked a flake of brown cardboard from her hair.

'Head and Boulders,' he said. 'That's what you need.'

'Get a life,' she said.

'It's a joke.'

'It's a habit,' she said. 'You say it all the time. It wasn't funny the first time. It's not funny now. You just keep repeating it. It's a habit. A very annoying habit.'

'As the bishop said to the nun,' he joked.

Carol banged her head on the glass counter. The charity box rattled. That's when it dawned on him. Maybe that's what was wrong. Maybe he and Linda had become a habit to each other. But what was wrong with that? Habits were things you liked. They were familiar, comfortable, reassuring.

He and Linda had been married for thirty-five years. They were bound to be familiar with each other after all that time. And comfortable, of course they were comfortable. They both worked. They only had one child. Comfortable with each other too. They both knew what each other thought about things. Sometimes they didn't agree but then they agreed to differ. They never argued. They'd been happy. That was reassuring, wasn't it?

Not any more, it wasn't. Obviously, Linda had decided he was a habit she could break. He was going to have to face this, have it out with her. It was the end of anything for a quiet life. No more Mister Nice Guy. He could break his own habits. He could rock the boat.

CHAPTER THREE

It wasn't so easy. By the time he got home, the kitchen smelled of warm pizza. A bottle of red wine was uncorked.

'All on your own?' he asked as Linda came down from the shower. The wet ends of her hair framed her face.

'Not any more,' she said, and planted a kiss on his cheek. The silk of her robe brushed his hand. She smelled of lavender soap. Not any more? What did that mean? Did she mean because he'd come in. Or did she mean Emilio? And why did she always shower before he came home? She had a shower every morning too.

'You take a lot of showers,' he said, grim faced.

'Have you only just noticed?' She poured the wine, handed him a glass, smiled.

'I notice a lot of things,' he said. 'You work in

an office.'

She laughed. She was so pretty when she laughed.

'Ten out of ten,' she said.

'That's not dirty work.'

'I feel dirty,' she said. 'Handling all those briefs.'

Everything she said sounded smutty. It sounded as if she was dropping hints. Did she want him to guess? He didn't have to guess. He knew.

'I know,' he said, pointedly.

'Then why are you fussing?' She opened the oven door. 'Pizza's ready.'

'I *know*,' he said again, even more pointedly.

'Then sit down,' she said, sliding the pizza onto a plate.

This wasn't working. Linda was acting as if everything was normal. She didn't even seem to notice how strange their conversation was. He'd have to be blunt. He sat down. She sat down. She pushed the pizza over to him. He took a slice. She pushed the salad bowl over. He helped himself. She started to eat.

'So, what did you get up to today?' he asked, as

bluntly as he could.

'Today was funny,' she giggled. 'Really funny.'

'Funny to you,' he said. 'It might not be so funny to me.'

'Oh, it will,' she laughed. 'We had this man come in. He wanted to fight a speeding ticket. Got flashed by a camera. He said it was the guy behind.' She choked laughing. 'Get that. It was the guy behind him who was speeding.'

Jas didn't get it. He was thinking about pizza. He was eating pizza. Pizza was Italian. He looked at the wine. Chianti. That was Italian too. Emilio was an Italian name. He'd even sounded Italian.

'What's all this Italian stuff about?' he asked.

'Goes together,' Linda said. 'Though I think pizza's really American.'

'*He's* Italian, isn't he?' Jas said. Let's see you get out of that, he thought.

'Who, the guy with the speeding ticket?' How could she look so innocent? 'No. What on earth made you think that?'

It was no good. He needed help. He just couldn't say it. The man who was in bed with you this morning. He needed a self-help book, that's what he needed. How to accuse your wife of cheating on you. The problem was he didn't want to say it out loud. It was bad enough thinking it. It was even worse knowing it. He didn't want to have to say it. He wanted her to say it. She was the one doing it. She should tell him, not the other way round.

'What made you think he was Italian?' Linda was frowning at him.

'Sounded like it to me,' Jas said.

'Because he was driving fast? Lots of people drive too fast. I hope you're not becoming racist. We're going to spend a lot of time over there.'

Jas wasn't feeling too happy about that any more. Maybe visiting their daughter in Tuscany had caused this. Maybe that's where Linda got this thing about Italian men. Maybe long holidays in Tuscany were a bad idea.

He sipped his wine. It was light, fruity. Wine? Was she trying to get him drunk? Maybe she thought he'd fall asleep. Maybe she wanted to sneak out. Worse. Maybe she wanted to sneak her other man in. Again. Twice in the one day. He looked across the table at her, his eyes narrow.

'What's with the wine?' he asked.

'It's Tuesday,' she said, as if that explained it.

'So?'

'Oh, come on. That means it's Wednesday tomorrow. You open an hour later. You get an hour extra in bed. *And* you have the afternoon off.' She said all this as if she expected him to understand, as if it would suddenly click. Nothing clicked.

'So?' he said again.

'So we always ... On Tuesday nights ... You like to ... Every Tuesday. Jas, we always have wine on Tuesdays. Because we always ... you know.'

Have sex, that's what they always did Tuesday nights. He remembered now. He remembered but he couldn't believe she wanted to. Not now. She'd been in bed with one man already today. With *another* man. Now she wanted to jump into bed with her husband. Had she no shame?

'You shameless hussy,' he said.

She laughed. She actually laughed.

'You wish,' she said.

CHAPTER FOUR

Jas needed help. Now he really needed help. His wife was cheating on him. That was bad enough. Now he'd cheated on himself. She'd slept with another man. Then he'd slept with her too. His own wife. How could he? How could he have sex with her after she'd slept with someone else? Had he no shame? No. That was the answer. No, he had no shame. He had no pride. He was a wimp. A total and utter wimp.

All Wednesday morning he'd been thinking about it. All morning, the more he thought about it, the worse he felt. Carol didn't work Wednesdays so he was alone with his bad feelings. The customers didn't seem to notice he wasn't his usual cheery self. In fact, they even seemed glad to be served without one of his cheery little jokes. Some of them even used his silence to turn the tables.

'Penny for them,' Brian Robertson said, then before Jas could answer, he stopped him. 'Naw, why waste a penny? Stick it in the charity box. It'll go to good use then.' And he went off chuckling.

Yip, Jas was a joke. The local joke. They all knew. They knew he was a wimp. Knew his wife was cheating on him. Thought he was daft for putting up with it. And they didn't know the half of it. He'd done more than put up with it. He'd done it with her too. His wife was cheating on him with another man. Now she was cheating on the other man with him, her husband. Something had to be done.

By the time Jas locked up the shop at lunchtime, he knew what he was going to do. He didn't get in his white van. Instead he walked out of the village. He turned left then took the fork up the back road to the canal bridge. As he walked he picked up stones and put them in his jacket pockets. When all his jacket pockets were full, he filled his trouser pockets.

By the time he reached the bridge, he had thighs like a boxer. All the stones in his trouser pockets made his thighs look and feel huge. It was difficult climbing up onto the parapet of the bridge. It was even harder to stand up on it without falling over the edge. Once he was standing, he pulled the belt out of his trousers and wound it round his wrists. He pulled the end of the belt through the middle with his teeth. Now he wouldn't be able to swim. Now he couldn't try to save himself. Now he was ready to jump.

He looked down at the water below. There was a barge coming. He smiled. Last time he'd shut his eyes. He hadn't seen the barge then. When he'd jumped, he'd gone down through its roof. He didn't want two broken legs again. He wanted to die.

This time there would be no mistake. This time, he'd wait till the barge passed. He'd wait till it was well past and the passengers wouldn't hear the splash. Then he'd jump. He dropped his bound hands down in front of him. They rested, tied, against his groin. He made himself look casual. He looked around at the trees, the clouds, the fields.

If the people on the barge saw him standing up above them on the stone parapet of the bridge, they'd think he was admiring the view. He swayed a little. The stones in his pockets were heavy. He didn't want to unbalance and fall in by accident. Not while the barge was passing underneath. He leaned back a little.

Against his thighs, his pockets started to slide downwards. The stones were stretching them. The catch on his trousers popped open. The stones slid further down his thighs. His trouser zip peeled apart. The stones pulled his pockets down to his knees. His trousers went with them.

Jas grabbed for the waistband to stop the slide. But his hands were tied together with his belt. He missed. His trousers slid down over his hips. He grabbed lower. He was too late. It was his boxers he grabbed. The trousers were round his ankles.

Horrified, Jas looked down at the barge. It was right below him. On it, an old woman stared back up at him. He knew what she could see. She could see a middle-aged man standing on the parapet above her, trousers round his ankles, clutching his privates with both hands. Her eyes grew wide. Her mouth grew wider. She raised her right hand and pointed at him. Then she screamed.

Jas saw every face on the barge look up at him.

They could all see. They all saw what she saw. Him, standing on the parapet, trousers round his ankles, clutching his privates. Jas jumped.

He jumped backwards onto the road. He hauled his hands out of the belt that bound them. He dragged his stone-filled trousers up. Then he stumbled and ran, throwing stones out of his pockets as he went. He ran all the way back to the shop and into his van.

Safe inside it, he threw the belt onto the passenger seat, started up and roared down the slope and out of the village. As he passed the fork in the road, men from the barge were running up the canal bank onto the road. Jas put his foot down and roared off round the canal turn and up the hill towards home.

CHAPTER FIVE

Inside his house, Jas gasped for breath, cursed, and pulled the last stones out of his pockets. He threw them, clattering, into the bin. He couldn't believe how stupid he'd been. He'd tried to jump in the canal once before in his life. It hadn't worked then. He should have known it wouldn't work now.

Tired of it all, he let his trousers drop to the kitchen floor. He kicked his shoes off and stepped out of the trousers, leaving them lying in a heap. He shrugged his jacket off and dropped it across a chair back. In his socks, boxers and shirt, he climbed the stairs. His feet sank into the thick stair carpet. He needed to lie down. He needed to rest.

The bedroom door was open. The bed was neatly made. Linda was such a tidy woman. She never left anything lying around. He lay down on top of the bed, stretched out, shut his eyes. Wednesday afternoon. It was the one time he had the house to himself. He could sleep, forget what had happened at the canal, forget his wife was having an affair. Just sleep. Only he couldn't. He could still see that old woman's face as she looked up at him from the barge.

Music. Some music would help. He stretched over to Linda's side of the bed. She kept her CD player there. She liked soft, easy listening music. He switched the CD player on, lay back against his pillow and shut his tired eyes.

'Cara mia,' Emilio's voice said. 'Cara mia.' Jas jumped upright, wide awake. It was Emilio all right. There was no mistaking that voice. It was the kind of voice to stroke a cat with. It rolled across the bed like melting chocolate. Jas had no idea what was being said. But it sounded sexy, suggestive. And it was coming from the CD. Jas wriggled over and switched it off.

A CD? She had Emilio's voice on a CD! Couldn't she get enough of the man in person? Did she have to listen to him even when he wasn't there? Jas got out of bed and paced around the room. It felt as if Emilio was still there. In the room. It didn't feel like Jas's bedroom any more. It was Emilio's bedroom. What did this man have that Jas didn't, apart from a sexy Italian voice? Apart from Linda.

Jas couldn't work it out. What did Linda get from this Emilio that she didn't get from him? She didn't get Jas's voice on a CD, that's what she didn't get. She'd never asked Jas to record himself for her. She didn't listen to her husband's voice when he wasn't there. She rather have an Italian talk dirty to her than listen to her own husband whispering sweet nothings. Well, not any more!

Jas pressed eject on the CD player. He'd smash the CD into pieces. He reached out to remove it. Then he stopped. It was evidence. The CD was evidence of her affair. Now he could accuse Linda. She wouldn't be able to deny it. Not with the evidence there for anybody to hear. He pushed the CD drawer shut.

Then he wondered if there was any other evidence hidden in the bedroom. There might be notes, letters, maybe a diary. There might be things this Emilio had given his wife. Sexy presents. Jas padded over to Linda's underwear drawer and yanked it open. He'd never ever looked in this drawer.

It was stuffed full of her bras and briefs. Sensible, pretty but normal. Nothing Jas hadn't seen before. Except, right at the back, under everything else, there were some crisp new packets. Jas pulled them out. Silky things slid out of them. Skimpy things. Slinky reds, blacks, purples. He'd never seen Linda wear such colours. He'd never seen Linda wear so little!

Now he was on a hunt. He pulled open every drawer. He searched through her wardrobe. There was nothing different about her clothes. He crossed to her bedside table and pulled open the drawer. Skin cream. Night cream. Headache pills. Ha! That was a joke. A sick joke. She didn't have time for headaches. She had two men to cater for. No wonder she had a drawer full of pills.

Massage oil. He stared at the small bottle. Massage oil. What did she use that for? Jas would have liked a massage sometimes. Some days, having his back and shoulders rubbed would be just the thing after a hard day in the shop. Linda had never given him a back rub. This Emilio obviously got the back rubs and massage!

Jas put the bottle of massage oil down and reached right to the back of the drawer. His fingers touched something soft but firm. Something that felt a bit like jelly except, except it was long and thick and ... He pulled it out.

'Ahhh!' he yelled and dropped it. It fell with a thud onto the carpet. Then it just lay there, pinkly. It was ... It was ... He couldn't believe what it was. He didn't want to look at it but he couldn't take his eyes off it. He still had his, attached. He knew that. But his right hand touched his groin anyway, just to check. Of course it wasn't his. This, this thing on the carpet, was some other man's.

Sweat stood out on Jas's forehead. Sweat rolled down his cheeks. Then he realized. There was no blood. No sign of ugly cuts. This, this thing on the carpet, was neatly finished off. It was, it was plastic. That was a relief.

Jas sagged onto the bed. His legs were shaking. It was a toy. Gingerly, he picked it up. It didn't really look real. Not close up, it didn't. He'd lifted it by the bottom end. The end which had a flat bottom. It made him feel quite strange, holding it. He gave it a squeeze. There was a buzz. It throbbed in his hand.

'Ahhh!' he yelled and dropped it again. It stopped buzzing as soon as he let go. Now he knew what it was. The way it looked. The way it buzzed. The way it had throbbed in his hand, vibrating. It was a toy all right, a vibrator. A sex toy.

It was one of those, those things, sold in sex shops. Shops that said 'For Adults Only'. Jas didn't feel adult enough to look at it any longer. He bent over, grabbed it by the other end this time, and shoved it back in the drawer. He shoved it right back into the back of the drawer and shut it.

Next, he gathered up all the new silky, slinky underwear. Maybe they came from the same kind of 'Adults Only' shop. He shoved them back into Linda's underwear drawer. He tried to be careful. He didn't want Linda to know he'd seen them. Not now. Not after that, that thing. He pushed them all back under everything else, just the way they had been. Then he went downstairs.

CHAPTER SIX

Downstairs, Jas poured himself a whisky. He needed a stiff drink. His nerves were in tatters. The things that had been going on in his house! Some strange Italian man that Jas didn't even know was sleeping with his wife. Sleeping with his wife in his bed in his bedroom! Some sex-mad Italian was buying his wife sexy underwear. They rubbed each other with massage oil! They used sex toys!

Jas downed the whisky. He couldn't imagine the things they were getting up to. He didn't want to imagine. Another man had taken over from him. Taken over his wife, his bed, his bedroom. Maybe he'd even been in every room in the house. Jas had been married to Linda for thirty-five years. His wife had been pleasant, loving, well behaved. He loved her. He could take her anywhere. Now, at this time of life, he'd found out the truth. She was a wicked woman. Wicked!

Jas poured another whisky and downed it. Then he went back upstairs to the drawer in Linda's bedside table. He took out the strip of pills and shut it. His dreams of a happy retirement had gone. Thoughts of warm, fun winters in Tuscany in their daughter's house had gone. Linda would leave him. That was obvious. She would take her Italian to Tuscany. He'd know the language. He'd show her round, take her places, talk to people. Jas couldn't match that.

Back downstairs, he took the whisky into the kitchen. He was sure Emilio had probably never been in the kitchen. Didn't come home for his tea yet. Hadn't quite got his feet under the table. The strip of pills had about twenty in it. That would be enough. He'd read warnings. It was dangerous to take any extra painkillers. It only took a few. That was the way to go. A bottle of whisky and a handful of pills. No pain. Just a nice drunk slide into sleep and away. That was the way to go.

He'd only taken four when his eyes began to feel heavy. Or maybe it was six. The whisky was making him lose track. He poured more, took another two pills. His head was heavy. He better take more pills. He reached for them. His head dropped onto his arm. He slouched on the table. His eyes closed. He was done for, out of it.

Pain woke him. He hadn't expected that. It shot across his gut. Jas jerked upright. A red-hot knife jabbed through him. Well, no pain, no gain. He gritted his teeth. Pain stabbed right through his middle. Then, like a big hand, it grabbed his stomach and squeezed. Then it twisted. Jas twisted in the chair. He yelled. He doubled over. He could hardly breathe.

Below his stomach, his gut growled like a mad dog. It was making more noise than him and he was making a lot of noise. This was pain. This was real pain. Having a baby couldn't be more painful. The great big hand that had a hold of his insides squeezed tighter and tighter. Jas had to run. Bent double, he ran upstairs to the bathroom.

In the bathroom, he was glad he only had his boxers on. He'd never have got his trousers down in time. He dived onto the toilet and sat there, doubled over. In agony. There was a great roar and all his insides came out into the toilet. At least that's how it felt. He was dying. He was dying and it hurt! Oh, God, how it hurt.

When Linda arrived home after work, the house seemed empty. The smell of whisky was everywhere.

'Jas, I'm home,' she called out. There was no answer. She hung her jacket up and went into the kitchen. It was empty. Jas's jacket was slung over the back of a chair as if he'd thrown it there in a hurry. On the floor there was a heap of his shoes and trousers. On the table sat the bottle of whisky. There was a half-full glass beside it. Next the glass was a strip of pills. There was a noise on the stair. A groan.

Linda went out into the hall. Jas was feeling his way down the stairs.

'There you are,' she said.

'Oohh,' he groaned.

'You look a bit pale,' she said.

'Aahhh,' he moaned, taking another step down.

'Feeling a bit bunged up, are you?' she asked.

'Aawww,' he sagged against the wall.

'I see you've taken some laxatives,' she said. 'That'll help you go.'

'Oh, oh, oh,' Jas said. Then he turned and

hurried back upstairs. The bathroom smelt like a whisky distillery. He only just made it.

Half an hour later, Linda was waiting for him in the kitchen. He crept in, still doubled over and slid onto a chair. She put a tall glass of cold water in front of him.

'Here. You had better drink this.'

He surely had. He had a raging thirst.

Linda lifted the strip of pills.

'How many of these did you take?' she asked.

'Two or three. A few.' His gut growled.

'You're supposed to take one,' his wife said. 'One at night. One in the morning. You'll be on the toilet for ever.'

He had been, ever since he woke. He didn't need anybody telling him what would happen. He knew. The fist that had a grip of his insides squeezed again.

'I took loads,' he said. 'I don't know how many. A handful.'

'Oh, Jas,' Linda said, worried. 'Don't you know by now? More isn't better.'

CHAPTER SEVEN

More isn't better. How could she say that? More was obviously better for her. She had one man to work and bring home the bacon. Then she had another man for sexy underwear, massage oil and sex toys. More was better for her, all right.

Not for Jas. More wasn't better for him. He tossed and turned all night. He made a lot of visits to the toilet. He drank lots of water. In the morning, his insides felt like they'd been chewed by a dog. A hungry dog with sharp teeth. A Dobermann.

It was all Linda's fault. If she'd left the pills in their packet, he would have seen what they were. Of course he was going to think they were headache pills. What other kind of pills would a woman her age keep next her bed? The whole thing was Linda's fault. You just couldn't trust women. He was a bit old to learn new tricks. But he'd learned that much.

'Women!' he said to Carol when she arrived at the shop. 'You can't trust them.'

'I'm on time,' she said. 'I'm always on time. Why are you standing like that?'

'Like what?'

'Sort of … twisted.'

'I am not.'

'You are.' She went to hang her coat through the back. 'Suits you, mind,' she said from off. At least that's what he thought she said.

'What pills do you keep beside your bed?' he asked when she came back through.

'Headache pills, of course,' she answered.

'I knew it!' Jas shouted with joy. He was right. 'Trust a woman,' he said.

Carol cocked her head on one side.

'You just said you couldn't.'

'When?'

'When I came in. On time. As usual. You said you can't trust women. Now you can trust them. Twisting that around took you less than five minutes.'

'You can't trust them for the big things,' Jas

said. 'You can only trust them for the small things. Like having a secret stash of headache pills. And some of them can't even be trusted for that. Excuse me.'

He headed through the back to the toilet. Carol watched him go. Then she picked up one of the morning papers and opened it at the jobs page.

After the morning rush of customers coming in for their papers and milk, Jas put the kettle on and made coffee.

'You still look a bit twisted,' Carol said, as they drank it.

He felt twisted. His gut was twisted. His heart was twisted. His head was twisted. There was a story in the papers about a man who'd stepped off the railway platform in front of a train. Jas wondered how many other ways he'd tried first.

'Your Linda doesn't look like a woman who gets headaches,' Carol said.

'What are you suggesting?'

'I'm not suggesting anything. She always looks bright and cheerful. Maybe that's why she doesn't have a stash of headache pills.'

'Meaning?' He knew what she was meaning. Women used headaches as an excuse. Linda never made excuses. Not even with strangers. Not even with Italian strangers. 'Meaning what?' he repeated.

Carol was losing it.

'Meaning the next time you go through to the toilet,' she snarled. 'See if you can flush yourself down the pan.' She went through the back then.

Jas heard the sound of cardboard boxes being ripped up. It sounded like a Dobermann was through there, ripping and snarling. Maybe Carol had a headache. Something was getting to her. Jas didn't care. He read again the story of the man who'd jumped in front of the train. Poor bloke. The people on the platform had all been shocked. But at least he'd made sure.

When Carol came back through, she had lumps of brown cardboard in her hair. Before Jas could speak she raised a warning finger at him.

'Say one word about Head and Boulders,' she warned.

He didn't. He didn't have to. She'd said it for him. Habits could be broken. He went to the toilet instead. His life, the life he'd planned, the life after the shop. It was over. He was all done. He just hadn't come to an end yet. But, as soon as he could stay out of the toilet for more than five minutes, he'd do something about that. Maybe he'd jump under a train. Third time lucky.

If only he hadn't gone back for his keys that morning, he wouldn't even know about Emilio. He'd still be planning his retirement. With Linda. In Tuscany. He'd still be a happy man.

Linda was still a happy woman. It was Thursday. Jas worked late on Thursdays. She had a whole extra two hours to herself before he'd come home. As she let herself into the empty house, she clutched her bag to her side in excitement. She flicked the lights on. Emilio was not going to be pleased. She didn't care. He'd served his purpose. Now she was going to retire him. She could always pick him up again another time.

Upstairs, she peeled off her working clothes. She hung the suit in the wardrobe and put her shirt and undies in the wash. Then she put her robe on. She'd have a shower. She'd been thinking about it all day. The first time was always more fun in the shower. But she'd better sort Emilio out first. She sat down on the edge of the bed.

'Emilio,' she said. 'It's been great. But we both knew it wouldn't last forever. I won't forget. And I will come back to you. But, right now, I need a change.' She flipped open the CD drawer and took out the CD. 'You sexy thing,' she said. She lifted her bag up beside her, opened it and took out the small book that went with the CD. *Learn Italian* it said on the cover. *Lesson 3: the language of love.* She slid the CD into its pocket and popped the book back into her bag.

'Ciao, Emilio,' she said. 'Bye.'

CHAPTER EIGHT

'Look,' Carol said. 'You're not fit to serve on your own anyway. What if customers come in and you're on the toilet?'

'You don't mind staying on?' Jas was relieved.

'Not if you pay me,' Carol said. 'I'll lock up. You can trust me, remember? I'm in early tomorrow anyway. Now you get away home.'

Home was exactly where Jas was planning to go. His body was a wreck. His head was a wreck. He knew what he had to do. He had to stop thinking about it. Tuscany, with Linda, would be much more fun than jumping in front of a train. He would go home and talk to his wife. Surely, once she knew that he knew, she'd stop seeing Emilio. He might not be that important to her. A fling, he might just be a fling.

Jas could forgive and forget. He was a big

enough man to do that, surely? Thinking about it made him feel better already. They could put the whole thing behind them. Turn over a new leaf. Start fresh.

It was dark outside now. He drove out of the village with the glimmer of hope in his heart and the beginning of a smile on his mouth. Halfway up the hill he began to whistle.

In her bedroom, Linda pulled a new book out of her bag. *Learn French*, it said. *Lesson 3: the language of love.* Tenderly, she drew the CD out of its pocket.

'Hello, Jacques,' she said. 'Bonjour.'

She popped the CD into the drawer on the player then carried it out to the landing. There was a socket outside the bathroom door where she plugged it in. She slid the cable under the door as she carried the CD player into the bathroom with her. Carefully, she sat the machine down, well away from any splashing water. Then she swished the shower curtain shut, switched on the shower and stepped out of her robe. When the water was at the right heat, she switched on the CD and stepped into the shower.

'Bonjour,' the man on the CD said. 'Mon nom est Jacques.'

All the lights were on when Jas pulled up outside his house. Linda was home. Now he felt a little nervous. There was one big flaw in his plan. Emilio. Emilio might be here. Jas didn't feel strong enough to throw an Italian super-stud out of his house. He better check first. He locked the van and tiptoed up to the door. He tried the handle. It was locked. That wasn't a good sign.

It took all his courage to put the key in the lock and open the door. As soon as he did, he heard the shower. That was all right. That was a relief. Linda always locked the door if he wasn't in when she was having a shower. She must be alone.

Jas started up the stairs. Better let her know she wasn't alone now, that he'd come home early. Halfway up the stairs he heard a moan. It came from the bathroom. A loud, deep moan. No. This couldn't happen again. They were in the shower together! Jas wanted to turn around but his feet were frozen to the spot. Then it came again. A deep moan of pleasure.

'Jacques, oh Jacques.'

Jacques? Who the hell was Jacques? Then Jacques spoke.

'Ma cherie,' he murmured. 'Ma cherie.'

Jas's heart froze. Jacques kept speaking. It was a long time since Jas had heard any French but he knew what this was about. His wife was in the shower with a Frenchman. Not Emilio. Not an Italian. A Frenchman called Jacques. And they were making love!

Jas felt his legs give way. He sat down, hard, on the stair. From the bathroom, he could hear the sounds of lovemaking. He could hear his wife and her lover, her new lover, repeating words of love and passion to each other. Over and over, they repeated them. Linda's voice rose. Her moans came quicker, deeper.

Jas had to get out of here. Without caring if they heard, he slid down the stairs on his tender backside. At the bottom, he got up and out the house as fast as he could. Shutting the door behind him, he ran down the path to his van.

His hands shook as he started it up. He switched on the lights, screeched out of the village and drove like a demon down the hill. He didn't care any more what happened to him. His wife was cheating on him. Not just with one lover. She had two!

Jas might have known better. Thinking didn't change anything. There was no way to turn the clock back. Things could not go back to how they were. He *had* gone back for his keys that morning. He *did* know about Emilio. Now he knew about Jacques too. There was only one answer here. He had to stop going home. If he didn't, he'd probably find Falkirk football team queued up outside one day.

At the foot of the hill, he took the bend over the canal on two wheels. That made him slow down. He didn't want to go in the canal. He'd tried that. It didn't work for him. He knew where he was going and he wanted to stay alive long enough to get there.

CHAPTER NINE

Jas drove past the turn into his shop and on down towards the town. Halfway down, he took a left, drove a few more yards and pulled over. This was where he wanted to be, up above the High station. The trains to Edinburgh and Glasgow passed underneath the road here. A train was the way to be sure. A train would finish it. The man in the morning paper had proved that.

Underneath the road, the trains went into a tunnel. There was only one side to jump from. Jas leaned over the wall and looked down at the station. Under the platform lights, he could see people standing about. That meant there was a train due. The one from Glasgow would come first. It would come towards him.

He would see its lights coming round the bend towards the station. Then it would stop at the station. That would give him plenty of time to get up on the wall. He didn't want to be seen standing there. Some passing driver might try to be a hero and save him.

It wasn't a high wall. Only as high as his chest. But it had a narrow top. He didn't want to fall too soon either. It was a long way down but maybe not far enough to kill him. He could be left lying on the track, his back or legs broken. The train might go safely over the top of him. No, he'd have to time it just right.

He had a practice. Both arms flat on the top of the wall. A quick push. Yes, he'd get up there, no bother. Up there, and straight over. A quick fall through the air and – splatter! One good skelp with the front of the train. It would be so quick, he wouldn't feel a thing. He wouldn't even have time to think. That would be good.

He'd done enough thinking. His head was sore with it. His daughter might miss him. But she had a new home, a new husband and a new life. Carol might miss him. But not for long. She was looking for a new job anyway. The new owner of the shop might not keep her on. His wife? Well, Linda had Jacques to comfort her. And Emilio.

Falkirk Football Club for all Jas knew. She wouldn't miss him.

He heard a train coming. Lights came round the bend heading into the station. Jas got ready, both arms flat on the top of the wall. The train was at the station. It was going too fast to stop. It didn't stop! It shrieked towards him.

Jas hauled himself up. The train horn blew as it rattled towards the tunnel. Jas was up on the wall and, without stopping, threw himself over it. The train screeched into the tunnel. Jas fell down, down, down. Then everything stopped. He didn't hear the thump as he landed. He didn't feel the thump as he landed. He was out of it.

It was black. Very black. Jas felt sick. The world swayed about. His face was pressed against something rough, bumpy and hard. There was a roaring sound in his ears. A roaring, rattling sound. Jas blinked, coughed. He moved his hands. The stuff he was lying on was lumpy. Small lumps that felt hard but dusty. It had a smell he thought he knew. It was coal! He was in a coal truck. He was on a goods train, in a coal truck. And he wasn't dead.

He could feel wet trickling from his nose. It was bleeding. His chest was sore. He must have broken or bruised some ribs. Carefully, he moved each of his arms in turn. They hurt in places but he could move them and his hands. They weren't broken. He could feel his legs. He could move his feet. That meant his back wasn't broken either. Very carefully, he placed his hands flat on the coal and levered himself up onto his knees. He could move about.

Then he had a horrible thought. Maybe he *was* dead. Maybe there was an after-life after all. Maybe he was in hell. Or, at least, maybe he was in a coal truck that was heading for hell. Still on his knees, he scrambled to the edge of the truck and peered over. He saw shadowy trees, lights, houses. He knew where he was. It wasn't hell. It was Linlithgow. He was halfway to Edinburgh. And he was alive. Bruised, battered, bleeding but alive.

Not only was he alive, he was angry. All his life, he'd worked hard. He'd made a good life for his wife and daughter. They never wanted for anything. He'd been faithful, even when he'd been tempted. He was a good man, a good husband. Now look at the mess he was in. Stuck in a coal truck in the middle of the night hurtling towards Edinburgh. He wanted to go home. But if he tried to get out of this truck, he'd probably kill himself.

The rate the truck was travelling at changed. Jas was jerked away from the edge. The truck was slowing down. Was it going to stop? He'd no idea where goods trains stopped. They travelled faster than passenger trains. Maybe it was catching up on the train in front. It would have to slow down. It might even stop or go into a siding.

That is just what the train was doing. It slowed down to walking speed. It clicked, rattled and shunted over points. It came to a shuddering halt. Jas gripped the edge of the truck. He was just outside Linlithgow. He could see the street lights. Now he had to get out of the truck. More than that, he had to get out without being seen. The railway staff did not like people travelling without tickets. He could even get done for messing about on railway property.

When he heard doors opening and closing, he ducked down. He could hear men talking. Then the voices faded as the men walked away from the train. Jas peered over the edge of the truck again. It was dark. He could see nobody. He would be black and dusty from the coal. Chances were nobody would see him.

Grunting with pain from his cuts and bruises, he scrambled as quietly as he could over the side of the truck and dropped to the ground. He stood in its shadow and looked around to get his bearings. The centre of Linlithgow was over to his left. All he had to do was get there, and get a taxi.

CHAPTER TEN

There was a high chain fence around the goods yard. Climbing over it was not possible. Jas did not know whether to go left or right along it. He decided on left. At least then he'd be heading in the right direction. Eventually, the chain fence stopped and a wooden fence began. That was more like it. Jas found a spot where a pile of stones lay heaped against the fence. He climbed to the top of the pile, wriggled over the top of the fence and dropped down on the other side.

His ribs hurt more. His nose started bleeding again. But the ground was flatter here. More like road than field. There were large box shapes standing about. He walked between them, always heading for the bright lights of Linlithgow. As he walked, he wiped his nose with his sleeve. He was glad it was dark. He couldn't see what a mess he must look. He hoped, when he found a taxi, that the driver wouldn't notice either.

A growl stopped him in his tracks. Was that his gut still playing up? The growl came again. It was long, low and frightening. A dark shape moved from behind one of the piles of boxes. It was an animal shape with four legs. Jas peered at it in the dark. It was dog shaped. A big dog. It was a Dobermann! He must be in a goods yard. And this was the guard dog.

The dog growled, deep, long, seriously. Its eyes were red in the darkness. Its lip curled back, baring its teeth. Jas could see them shining white. Fine, he thought. He'd come all this way, broken and bruised, to bump into Carol in one of her box-ripping moods. Only the dog wasn't in a box-ripping mood. It was in a man-ripping mood. Even if he could run, which Jas couldn't, he'd never outrun it. All he could do was stand still and let it leap and rip his throat out. He was a dead man. After all he'd been through, he was a dead man.

The dog fixed its red eyes on Jas. It lowered its head and curled its lips back further off its teeth. It bent its back legs. Jas finally lost it.

'Come on then,' he shouted at it. 'Jump! Get it over with. Look, look.' He ripped his collar away from his neck. 'Here's my throat. Go for it. Come on, boy. Get it done. I don't care. Do you get it? I don't care any more.'

He started to laugh. He laughed wildly. His ribs ached with it. He laughed so hard he started to cry. Great sobs tore through him. He'd survived Linda, the canal, the laxatives and the train. Now he was going to be torn apart by a dog. And he didn't care. His wife was sleeping with a football team. He'd nothing left to live for anyway.

The dog stopped growling. It whined. It stopped crouching like a spring ready to leap. It circled about. It came over and nudged Jas with its nose. It whined again. Jas patted its head with his tear-stained, blood-soaked hand.

'I know, boy,' he said. 'You don't have much of a life either.'

The dog ran off and ran back with a stick. They had a growling tussle before Jas got the stick out of its mouth. The dog leapt around, growling in fun. Jas walked a few steps and threw the stick. It clattered behind some of the box shapes. The dog charged off. While it was gone, Jas hurried towards the fence.

When the dog came back with the stick, Jas stopped walking. They had the same tussle. The dog growled. Jas tugged at the stick. The dog let him have it. Jas walked on towards the fence a bit and threw the stick.

It took six throws to get across the yard to the fence at the other side. Jas threw the stick. The dog belted away after it. Jas pushed a box up to the fence. It scraped across the hard ground. The dog had heard the noise. It came back without the stick. It growled.

'Game's over, eh?' Jas said. 'Good boy.' He stepped up onto the box. The dog growled again. Its lip curled. Jas leapt for the top of the fence. The dog leapt for Jas. Jas grabbed the top of the fence. The dog grabbed his ankle. Its teeth bit into his skin. Jas kicked hard and pulled himself up. His trouser leg tore. The dog fell back. Jas threw himself over the fence. He fell with a splash on the other side. He was in a ditch.

Inside the fence, the dog growled and barked. Its claws scraped the wood. Jas thought it might come over but it didn't. He heard it whine then go away. Job done. It had seen him off. Now all he needed was a taxi. Jas stumbled out of the ditch, dripping wet. His ankle was sore and bleeding now too. He limped off towards the street.

Linda had turned the dinner down twice. She wondered what was keeping Jas. How on earth was he going to retire when he couldn't tear himself away from the shop? She was looking forward to it. Tuscany in the autumn. Spending more time with their daughter. Maybe they could stay all winter. There would be nothing to come home for, not till the weather got better. Winters in Tuscany. Linda liked the sound of that.

Jas was the only problem. He'd been acting very strange of late. He didn't seem to like the idea of Italy any more. The thought of giving up the shop must be getting to him. Maybe he wouldn't be able to do it. Maybe he didn't want to retire after all. She sighed. If he didn't get home soon, his dinner would retire.

She walked through to the hall and picked up the phone. She'd call the shop and tell him to lock up and come home. Now. She had just started to dial when she heard the car engine outside. That would be him now. Thank goodness.

As she turned towards it, the front door burst open. Jas stood there, black, bruised, blood stained, tattered and dripping.

'Jas,' she gasped. 'What happened?'

'I'll tell you what happened,' he said. 'Emilio happened, that's what. Jacques happened, that's what. They caused this. You happened. You, my wife! You did this!'

CHAPTER ELEVEN

Jas limped into the living room. He grabbed the whisky bottle and a glass and sat down, heavily, on the cream sofa.

'Jas, you're filthy.' Linda fussed into the room behind him.

'Oh,' he said. '*I'm* filthy, am I?' He poured himself a whisky.

'Yes,' Linda said. 'You're black.'

'Black not good enough?' Jas asked. 'Would brown be better? Well sorry. I don't do brown. I don't do Italian. I don't do French either. But I do know what's been going on here!' He downed the whisky and poured another.

'Nothing's been going on, Jas,' Linda said.

'Emilio's been going on, Linda. I *know*. So where is he tonight? I was working late, wasn't I? That's a good chance to see him. Except you were busy tonight, weren't you? Busy with Jacques! I came home early, Linda. You were in the shower with him. Gone, is he?'

'No. No, he's not gone.'

Jas choked on his whisky.

'Not gone?'

'No, he's still here. So's Emilio. Just wait there.' She left the room.

Jas couldn't believe it. She had both of them here at once. He was right. She was wicked. A wicked, wicked woman. No doubt, when she came back with the pair of them, Falkirk football team would be jogging right behind. Linda came back with her handbag. She knelt down on the cream carpet, sat the bag on the coffee table and opened it.

'There,' she said. 'That's Emilio.' She sat a small, thick book down in front of Jas. *Learn Italian*, it said on the cover. *Lesson 3: the language of love*. 'And that,' she took a second book from her bag. 'Is Jacques.' *Learn French*, this one said. *Lesson 3: the language of love*. She flipped the cover of the Italian book and drew a CD out of the pocket inside. 'Emilio,' she said. 'See?'

'No.' Jas was speechless.

'I wanted to surprise you. For our retirement,' she went on. 'If we're going to spend a lot of time in Italy, one of us should speak the language.'

'And the French? You can speak French already.' Something she was saying didn't fit but Jas couldn't work it out. Linda blushed.

'I just felt like a change. Thought I should brush up.'

'No, no, no.' Jas shook his head. 'You were in the shower. And,' he remembered. 'There's more.' He got to his feet and limped out of the room to the stairs. The cream sofa had a damp, dusty black stain where he'd sat.

Up in their bedroom, Jas yanked open Linda's underwear drawer. He pulled out the crisp new packets.

'What about this?' he asked. 'And this, and this.' Silky, slinky, sexy things spilled over the floor.

'That was to be another surprise,' Linda said. Her face went red again. Now they were getting somewhere.

Jas limped over to her bedside table. He hauled open the drawer.

'And this?' he said, pulling out the vibrator from the back of it. 'Was this going to be an even bigger surprise?' He threw it on the bed. The sex toy lay there. Pink, plastic and male. Linda went very red. She screwed her eyes shut.

'It's just for fun,' she said.

'Fun!' Jas was angry now. Really angry. 'Fun for you and your lovers!'

'No,' Linda shook her head. 'Alone.' She looked at him then. Straight into his eyes. 'Fun for me on my own.' She reached into the open drawer and lifted out the bottle of massage oil. 'And before you ask, I use that too. With … it.' She waved her hand towards the male object on the bed.

Surely, she didn't mean what she just said.

'So you do it on your own! Am I not enough fun for you?'

Linda folded her arms.

'Since you ask,' she said quietly. 'No. You're no fun at all. You just do this wham, bam, thank you, ma'am thing. You never think about me. When we have sex, it's only about you. I need some pleasure too.'

Jas sat down on the bed. His legs had gone

again. He was crusted in coal dust, mud and blood. And he was crushed. He was a fool. A silly, old fool.

'You never said anything.'

'How could I? I love you. I didn't want to hurt your feelings.'

That was something. She loved him.

'Thirty-five years, Linda,' he said. 'You've been unhappy for thirty-five years?'

'No.' She sat down on the bed beside him. 'I haven't been unhappy. I've been very happy. I enjoy pleasing you. Just, sometimes, I'd like to be pleased.'

He looked at her. At her lovely hair that was beginning to go grey. At her sweet, pretty face. He loved this woman. Pure and simple. He loved her. Okay, he was an old dog. But he wasn't that old.

'I could learn,' he said. 'If you would teach me.'

The doorbell rang. Linda smiled.

'You go and run a bath,' she said. 'I'll get that. And I'll take the dinner out the oven.'

Jas lay back on the bed. He'd been shocked, upset and scared. He was bruised, battered, bleeding. He looked like a dog's dinner. He'd almost been a dog's dinner. He'd almost lost everything. Linda, his daughter, Tuscany, his life. He'd been a first class fool. But it was all right now. Linda loved him. They were going to start again. They were going to learn new things, new tricks. They were going to be all right. He was a happy man. Linda came back into the room.

'Jas,' she said. She sounded worried.

Jas sat up. From behind Linda, two policemen came into the room.

'Mr Ferrier?' the first one asked. 'Mr Jas Ferrier?'

'Yes.' Jas tried to stand up but the pain in his bitten ankle was too sore. 'Sorry,' he said. 'I just can't …'

'That's all right, sir,' the policeman said. 'You look like you've been in the wars.' He was staring at something. Not Jas. Something on the bed beside Jas. It was the vibrator. Linda's sex toy.

Jas put his hand over it.

'Sorry, officer. We were just …' He shut up, picked the thing up. It buzzed and throbbed. Jas shoved it back into the drawer and shut it. He shouldn't have trusted Carol to lock up. All he needed right now was a break-in at the shop. He'd have to go there with them, check the stock, say what had been taken. 'What's this about, officer?' he asked.

'We've had a report,' the policeman said, 'of a flasher exposing himself to people on a canal barge. We'd like to talk to you about it.'

CHAPTER TWELVE

'Jas?' Linda looked horrified.

'It's all right, Linda. I can explain.'

'Good.' The policeman took out his notebook. 'Because we'd like to hear that, sir.'

The second policeman stepped forward.

'Are you the owner of a white van?' he asked, giving the make, model and number of Jas's van.

'Well, yes,' Jas said. The men he saw running up from the canal bank that day must've had good eyesight, and good memories.

The first policeman took over again.

'Would you like to tell me in your own words, sir? About that day at the canal.'

So Jas told the story. He tried to spare Linda as much as he could. She'd been learning Italian. He'd heard the man's voice on the CD and thought she was having an affair. He'd been so upset, he wanted to die. He'd gone down to the canal bridge. He filled all his pockets with stones so he'd sink not swim. He tied his hands with his belt and got up on the parapet of the bridge. A barge was coming so he stood there waiting. The weight of the stones had pulled his trousers down. That was all. He had his boxers on. He wasn't flashing anybody.

It all sounded okay to Jas. The policeman asked if that was the whole story. Jas thought long and hard. Yes, it was. He couldn't think of anything else. It was just a mistake. He could see why the people on the barge thought he was a flasher. But he wasn't. It was just a simple mistake.

'About your van,' the policeman said. 'We found it parked on the road above the High station.'

'It wasn't lost,' Jas said. 'I left it there.'

'Strange place to park, sir. When you live here.'

'I was going for a train,' Jas said.

'So you'll have your ticket, sir?' The second policeman asked.

'Eh, no. Sorry, there wasn't time to get one.'

The first policeman flipped over a few pages of his notebook. 'I have a report here,' he said, 'of a man climbing up onto the wall above the station. From the road where your van is parked. Did you see anyone?'

'No.'

'The description we have fits what you're wearing, sir. What's left of it.'

'All right, all right,' Jas said. 'That was me.'

'Jas!' Linda sounded shocked.

'The statements we have say the man disappeared quite quickly,' the policeman explained. 'Would you like to tell me what happened?'

So Jas told that story. He'd come home early. He'd heard a Frenchman in the shower with his wife.

'She's learning French too?' the officer asked.

'No,' Jas said. 'She can speak French. It was just to brush up.' He told what he thought he'd heard, Linda making love with a Frenchman. Emilio had been bad enough. He said how he felt thinking his wife now had two lovers. Then he told them how he'd driven to the station, climbed up on the wall and thrown himself in the path of the train.

He told them everything. How he came round in a coal truck. How he got out when the train stopped at Linlithgow. How he'd escaped from the dog. Everything.

'And then you came home and made up with your wife?'

'Yes.'

'You must be a very lucky man, sir.'

Jas smiled at Linda. She didn't smile back.

'Yes,' he said to the policeman. 'I am.'

'If you'd stood up on the wall above the station,' the second policeman said. 'The people on the platforms would have seen you.'

'Yes, they would.'

'So might some of the people on the trains.'

'I suppose.'

'If you hadn't fallen, what would you have done next?'

'I didn't fall,' Jas said. 'I jumped.'

'You didn't jump into the canal,' the officer said.

'No.'

'You didn't fall then either.'

'That's right.'

'You just dropped your trousers.'

'No!' Jas said. 'They slid down. I told you.'

'Do you have a thing about flashing people from bridges?' the officer asked.

'Good places for it,' the first policeman said. 'You're on the road above. Beside your van. You can get away without being caught.'

Linda gasped. She glared at Jas.

'And you had the cheek to question me,' she said.

Jas turned to her. She looked shocked. Shocked and disgusted. Everything they'd just found was disappearing again. Selling the shop. Retiring together. Tuscany. Learning new things. Doing new things.

'Linda, it's not like that. I said what happened.'

'You really expect me to believe all that?' she asked. 'Do I look stupid?'

Jas put his head in his hand. He was not a happy man. He sighed a deep sigh that hurt his ribs. All he had was the truth. Truth that sounded like lies. Sometimes, just sometimes, living was harder than dying. This was wicked. That's what it was. Wicked.

He turned back to the policeman.

'For God's sake, officer,' he said. 'Do I look

like a flasher?'

The policeman gave him a long look. He looked at the dirt, the bruises, the blood, the torn clothes. Then he opened the drawer of the bedside table and took out the sex toy. He put it into Jas's limp hands.

'Now, sir,' he said. 'You tell me what you look like.'

Published with this volume

WINNING THROUGH
Brian Irvine

In *Winning Through* Brian Irvine tells
the truth about his life as a footballer. From
family life in Airdrie we follow him as he
realises his boyhood dreams. He becomes an
international player with Aberdeen and Scotland.
But he has to cope with bad times, and worse,
when he is told he has a serious and possibly
fatal illness. Finally he has to come to terms
with the end of a long playing career. Brian's
Christian faith and strong family ties help him to
cope, and to 'win through'.

Brian Irvine was a professional footballer
with Falkirk, Aberdeen, Dundee and Ross
County. He represented Scotland nine times
before illness interrupted his career. When he
retired from playing he became Football
Development Officer with Ross County, a job
that includes community work in schools and
prison. He can often be heard giving his
expert comment on radio.

THE HIGHWAY MEN
Ken MacLeod

The weather has gone crazy and the war has spread to China.

Jase, Euan and Murdo are laggers: forced workers in a future Scotland. The laggers are helping to lay a new power line in the Highlands. Ailiss, a young woman from a secret settlement in the frozen hills, is going to strain their loyalties to breaking point – and beyond.

Ken MacLeod was born in Stornoway in 1954 and grew up in Greenock. He has worked at many jobs, from road-mending to computer programming. He is now a full-time writer and has written nine science fiction novels. He is married with two children and lives in West Lothian.

Also available

THE CHERRY SUNDAE COMPANY
Isla Dewar

THE BLUE HEN
Des Dillon

THE WHITE CLIFFS
Suhayl Saadi

BLOOD RED ROSES
Lin Anderson

GATO
Margaret Elphinstone

THESE TIMES, THIS PLACE
Muriel Gray

Moira Forsyth, *Series Editor for the Sandstone Vistas, writes:*

The Sandstone Vista Series of books has been developed for readers who are not used to reading full length novels, or for those who simply want to enjoy a 'quick read' which is satisfying and well written.